Ladybird Readers

The Pony
School News

Series Editor: Sorrel Pitts
Adapted by Sorrel Pitts

LADYBIRD BOOKS

UK | USA | Canada | Ireland | Australia
India | New Zealand | South Africa

Ladybird Books is part of the Penguin Random House group of companies
whose addresses can be found at global.penguinrandomhouse.com.
www.penguin.co.uk   www.puffin.co.uk   www.ladybird.co.uk

Penguin
Random House
UK

First published by 2018
001

Printed in China

A CIP catalogue record for this book is available from the British Library

ISBN: 978-0-241-31611-5

All correspondence to
Ladybird Books
Penguin Random House Children's
80 Strand, London WC2R 0RL

MIX
Paper from
responsible sources
FSC
www.fsc.org   FSC® C018179

Ladybird Readers

The Pony School News

Picture words

Sweetie
Belle

Scootaloo

Apple
Bloom

Diamond
Tiara

Twilight
Sparkle

Fluttershy

Applejack

Pinkie Pie

Featherweight

Snips and
Snails

bubble gum

diary

hug

pony mark

It was the first day of school, and Sweetie Belle and Scootaloo were not happy.

"Featherweight got his pony mark in the summer holidays!" said Scootaloo. "How can *we* get our pony marks?"

9

Then, Apple Bloom came.

"Did you hear about
Diamond Tiara?" she said.

"She has a new job at *The Pony School News*. We can write stories for her—then we can get our pony marks!" said Apple Bloom.

Diamond Tiara talked to
Sweetie Belle, Scootaloo,
Apple Bloom, and the other ponies.

"I have a lot of new ideas for
The Pony School News," she said.

Sweetie Belle, Scootaloo, and Apple Bloom wrote some stories for Diamond Tiara.

Apple Bloom wrote about Ponyville in the past. Scootaloo wrote about baby animals. Sweetie Belle wrote about her favorite hats.

They all gave their stories to Diamond Tiara, but she was angry.

"This isn't news," Diamond Tiara said. "Write some exciting stories!"

"How can we find interesting stories?" said Scootaloo.

Then, Sweetie Belle saw something that was funny. "Featherweight, take some photographs of this!" she said.

Snips and Snails both had bubble gum on their bodies!

The ponies wrote the story for *The Pony School News*.

They called it "Snips and Snails and Bubble Gum" by Gabby Gums. "Gabby Gums" was the ponies' newspaper name.

All the ponies laughed
when they read the story.

Snips and Snails were not
happy, but Diamond Tiara
was very happy!

"Let's write lots of Gabby Gums stories," said Sweetie Belle. "Then we can get our pony marks!"

Sweetie Belle, Scootaloo, and Apple Bloom wrote lots of stories about their friends' problems.

Some stories were funny,
but some were not.

Now, all the ponies in Ponyville wanted to read Gabby Gums's stories. They ran to the school shop to buy the newspaper.

Some ponies were not happy.

"I don't like these stories," said Twilight. "Gabby Gums is writing about our lives."

"I think Gabby Gums is really funny," said Applejack.

"Gabby Gums mustn't write about our friends' problems," said Twilight. "It's not right."

The other ponies laughed at her.
"We love reading about our
friends' problems!" they said.

Sweetie Belle, Scootaloo, and Apple Bloom didn't like writing about their friends.

"We want to write about other things, too," they told Diamond Tiara.

Diamond Tiara was angry. "Ponies only want to read Gabby Gums's stories," she said.

Soon, there was a new
Pony School News to read.

Applejack, Pinkie Pie, and
Fluttershy read it. They began
to feel angry, too. Now the
stories were about them!

TWILIGHT SPARKLE: "I'M
BETTER THAN OTHER PONIES!"

APPLEJACK IS
ALWAYS SLEEPING!

PINKIE PIE LIKES TO
HAVE TOO MUCH FUN!

FLUTTERSHY'S HAIR
IS TOO PINK!

Rarity went into her sister's room. Sweetie Belle had her diary!

"YOU are Gabby Gums!" Rarity said, surprised. "You write these terrible things!"

"Apple Bloom and Scootaloo write them, too," said Sweetie Belle. "We are ALL 'Gabby Gums'."

Rarity was very angry.

The other ponies stopped speaking to Sweetie Belle, Apple Bloom, and Scootaloo.

"We must say sorry,"
said Sweetie Belle.

Then, Sweetie Belle wrote a note in *The Pony School News*.

Dear Ponies,

We are sorry about our "Gabby Gums" stories.
We wrote them because we wanted our pony marks,
but we were wrong.

We hope you understand.
Please be our friends again.

From,
Sweetie Belle, Apple Bloom, and Scootaloo

The ponies read the note.
Diamond Tiara was very angry.
Now, no ponies wanted to read
The Pony School News!

"It's OK. We know you're sorry," the ponies said to Sweetie Belle, Apple Bloom, and Scootaloo.

Then, they gave them a big hug! It felt good to be friends again!

45

Activities

The key below describes the skills practiced in each activity.

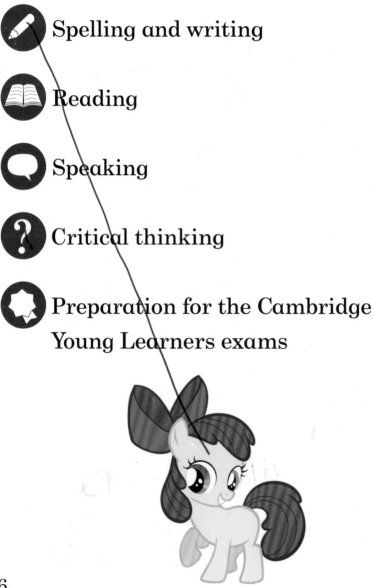

Spelling and writing

Reading

Speaking

Critical thinking

Preparation for the Cambridge Young Learners exams

1 Circle the correct pictures. 📖

1 These ponies were not happy on the first day of school.

a b c

2 This pony got a pony mark in the summer holidays.

a b c

3 This pony asked, "How can *we* get our pony marks?"

a b c

2 Look, match, and write the words.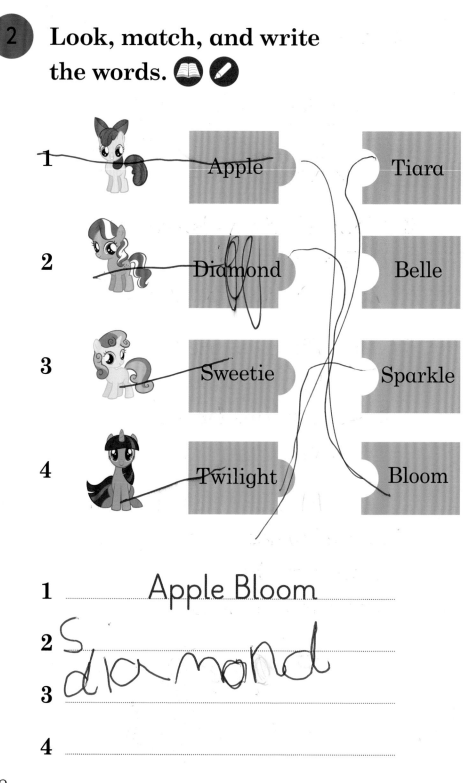

1	Apple	Tiara
2	Diamond	Belle
3	Sweetie	Sparkle
4	Twilight	Bloom

1 Apple Bloom

2 S

3 diamond

4

3 **Choose the correct answers.** 📖 ✿

1 Apple Bloom knew about

   a Diamond Tiara's new job.

   b Diamond Tiara's pony mark.

2 Diamond Tiara's job was at

   a *The Ponyville News.*

   b *The Pony School News.*

3 Apple Bloom wanted to

   a read a newspaper.

   b write stories for the
   school newspaper.

4 Apple Bloom and her friends
   wanted to get

   a pony marks.

   b jobs in the school.

4 Look and read. Put a ☑ or a ☒ in the boxes. 📖⭐

1  Sweetie Belle, Scootaloo, and Apple Bloom wrote some stories.

2  Apple Bloom wrote about her school.

3  Sweetie Belle wrote about her favorite hats.

4  Apple Bloom wrote about Ponyville today. ☑

5  Scootaloo wrote about baby animals. ☑

5 Read the questions.
Write complete answers.

1 Who wrote some stories for
Diamond Tiara?

Sweetie Belle, Scootaloo, and
Apple Bloom wrote some
stories for Diamond Tiara.

2 How did Diamond Tiara feel about
the stories?

SamHaABDLSiham

3 What did Diamond Tiara want?

6 **Write the missing letters.**

ee   oo   pp

1   Sw__ee__tie Belle

2   Sc__ __tal

3   A__ __le
       Bl__ __m

4   A__ __lejack

7 **Work with a friend. Look at the pictures. One picture is different. How is it different?** 💬 ❓

1 (a) (b) (c)

Picture c is different because Sweetie Belle is not sad.

2 (a) (b) (c)

3 (a) (b) (c)

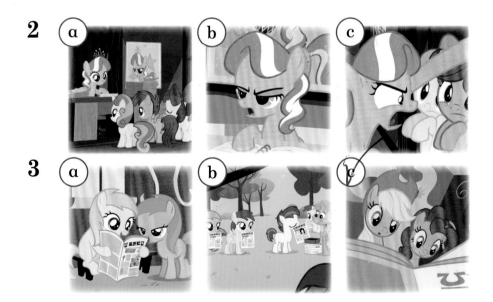

8 **Look and read. Write _T_ (true) or _F_ (false).**

1 All the ponies laughed when they read the story. ....T..........

2 Snips and Snails laughed at the story, too. ....

3 Diamond Tiara did not like Gabby Gums's story. ....

4 Gabby Gums's story was about other ponies' problems. ....

5 Diamond Tiara wanted more Gabby Gums stories. ....

9 Circle the correct words.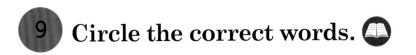

1 Sweetie Belle, Scootaloo, and Apple Bloom wanted ~~Snips and Snails~~ / **Diamond Tiara** to like their story.

2 Apple Bloom wanted to write stories to get **a pony mark. / new friends.**

3 Diamond Tiara wanted the ponies to write **exciting / angry** stories.

4 Some stories were **funny, / boring,** but some were not.

Find the words.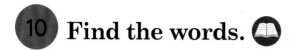

s	w	e	i	t	p	o	b	s
c	h	l	a	n	b	u	o	t
o	s	c	h	o	o	l	d	o
p	r	o	b	l	e	m	i	r
i	n	g	a	d	d	i	e	i
e	p	o	n	i	e	s	s	e
t	o	m	x	q	o	w	k	s

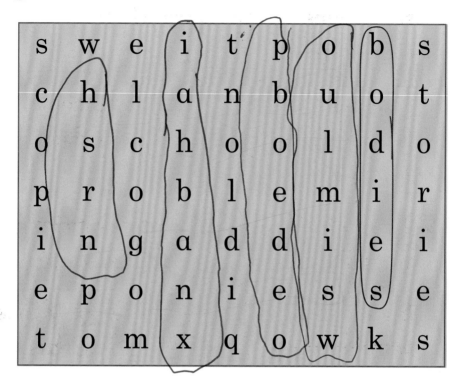

bodies   school   ponies

stories   problem

11 Match the two parts of the sentences. Then, write them on the lines. 📖 ✏️

1 Sweetie Belle, Scootaloo, and Apple Bloom

2 Their stories were about

3 Some stories were funny,

a but some were not.

b wrote lots of stories.

c other ponies' problems.

1 Sweetie Belle, Scootaloo, and Apple Bloom wrote lots of stories.

2

3

12 **Read the story. Choose the correct words and write them next to 1—3.**

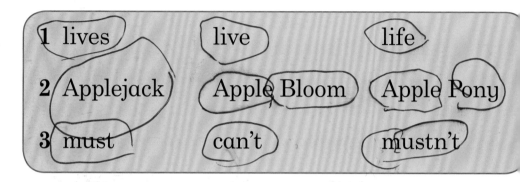

1 ~~lives~~   live   life

2 ~~Applejack~~   ~~Apple Bloom~~   ~~Apple Pony~~

3 ~~must~~   ~~can't~~   ~~mustn't~~

1 "Gabby Gums is writing about our

_____lives_____," said Twilight.

2 "I think Gabby Gums is really funny,"

said _____.

3 "Gabby Gums _____

write about our friends' problems,"

said Twilight.

13 **Read the questions. Write answers using words in the box.** 📖 ✏️ ❓

| sleeping | fun | Twilight Sparkle |

1 Why did Applejack not like the story about her?

The story said that she was always sleeping.

2 Which pony did not like the story "I'm better than other ponies"? Why?

K ℞ ₁

3 What did the story say Pinkie Pie had too much of?

14 Look and read. Choose the correct words and write them on the lines.

Rarity ~~diary~~ ~~hug~~ ~~Gabby Gums~~

1 This pony is Sweetie Belle's sister. _____Rarity_____

2 This is a book that you write in. _____R_____

3 This was the newspaper name of the three ponies. _____Rarity_____

4 Fluttershy gave the ponies one of these. _____

Diamond Tiara was very angry. Now, no ponies wanted to read her newspaper.

1 Sweetie Belle, Apple Bloom, and Scootaloo wanted to say sorry.

The ponies said, "It's OK. We know you're sorry."

Sweetie Belle wrote a note in *The Pony School News*.

Then, the other ponies gave them a big hug!

16 Talk to a friend about Gabby Gums's stories.

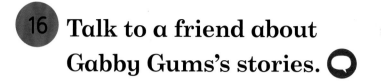

1 Who wrote the Gabby Gums stories?

Sweetie Belle, Scootaloo, and Apple Bloom wrote them.

2 Why did they write these stories?

3 Why did the other ponies stop speaking to Sweetie Belle, Apple Bloom, and Scootaloo?

4 Why did Sweetie Belle write a note in *The Pony School News*?

17 **Write the questions.** 📖 ✏️

1 (into) (room) (Who) (her) (went) (sister's) (?)

Who went into her sister's room?

2 (a) (Who) (diary) (had) (?)

Who had a diary

3 (was) (angry) (Who) (?)

Who was angry

4 (these) (things) (Who) (wrote) (terrible) (?)

5 (Gabby) (Are) (Gums) (you) (?)

WLRGFABDVV

Level 3

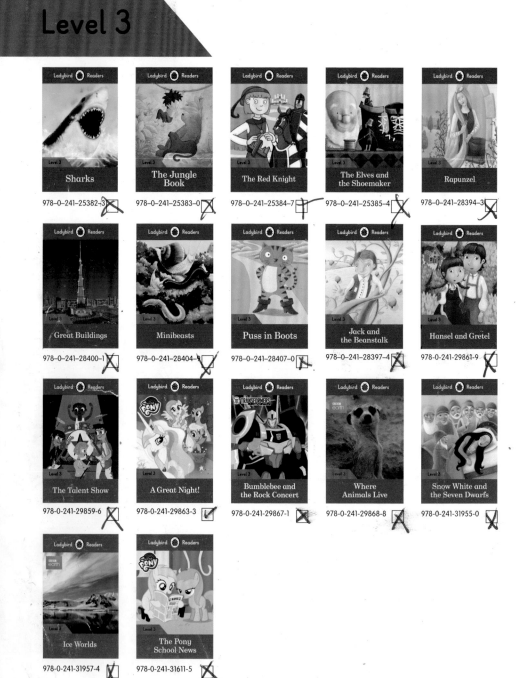

Sharks	The Jungle Book	The Red Knight	The Elves and the Shoemaker	Rapunzel
978-0-241-25382-3	978-0-241-25383-0	978-0-241-25384-7	978-0-241-25385-4	978-0-241-28394-3
Great Buildings	Minibeasts	Puss in Boots	Jack and the Beanstalk	Hansel and Gretel
978-0-241-28400-1	978-0-241-28404-9	978-0-241-28407-0	978-0-241-28397-4	978-0-241-29861-9
The Talent Show	A Great Night!	Bumblebee and the Rock Concert	Where Animals Live	Snow White and the Seven Dwarfs
978-0-241-29859-6	978-0-241-29863-3	978-0-241-29867-1	978-0-241-29868-8	978-0-241-31955-0
Ice Worlds	The Pony School News			
978-0-241-31957-4	978-0-241-31611-5			

Now you're ready for Level 4!